D1120112

Dedicated to families everywhere,
especially mine!

—CHRISTINE TAYLOR-BUTLER

For my three daughters
Lonique, Lonaya, and Lonae

—LONNIE OLLIVIERRE

Reycraft Books
55 Fifth Avenue
New York, NY 10003
Reycraftbooks.com

Reycraft Books is a trade imprint and trademark of Newmark Learning, LLC.



Library of Congress Control Number: 2021902245

ISBN: 978-1-4788-7063-0

Printed in Dongguan, China. 8557/0521/17948
10 9 8 7 6 5 4 3 2 1

Author photo courtesy of Christine Taylor-Butler
Illustrator photo courtesy of Lonnie Ollivierre

First Edition Hardcover published by Reycraft Books

Reycraft Books and Newmark Learning, LLC. support diversity, the First Amendment and celebrate the right to read.

# The Get-Together

BY **Christine Taylor-Butler**

ILLUSTRATED BY **Lonnie Ollivierre**

Today is my

Great Uncle Wesley's 95th birthday.

This year, like every year before,

family travels far and wide in celebration.

Black eyed peas,
greens and cornbread,
pineapple hams,
and buttermilk biscuits
cover tables, end to end.

Is that **macaroni and cheese** I see?

# Aunt Birdie's fabulous carrot cake

towers above it all,
dripping mounds
of cream cheese frosting.

Aunt Thelma slides her
brick-hard fruitcake
to the front of the table.

“Going to have some?” I ask.

“I may be old, but I’m not crazy,”
says Uncle Wesley.

He winks and sprinkles
crumbs on his plate and mine.
“She’ll think we had a piece.”

Aunt Thelma beams as we walk by.

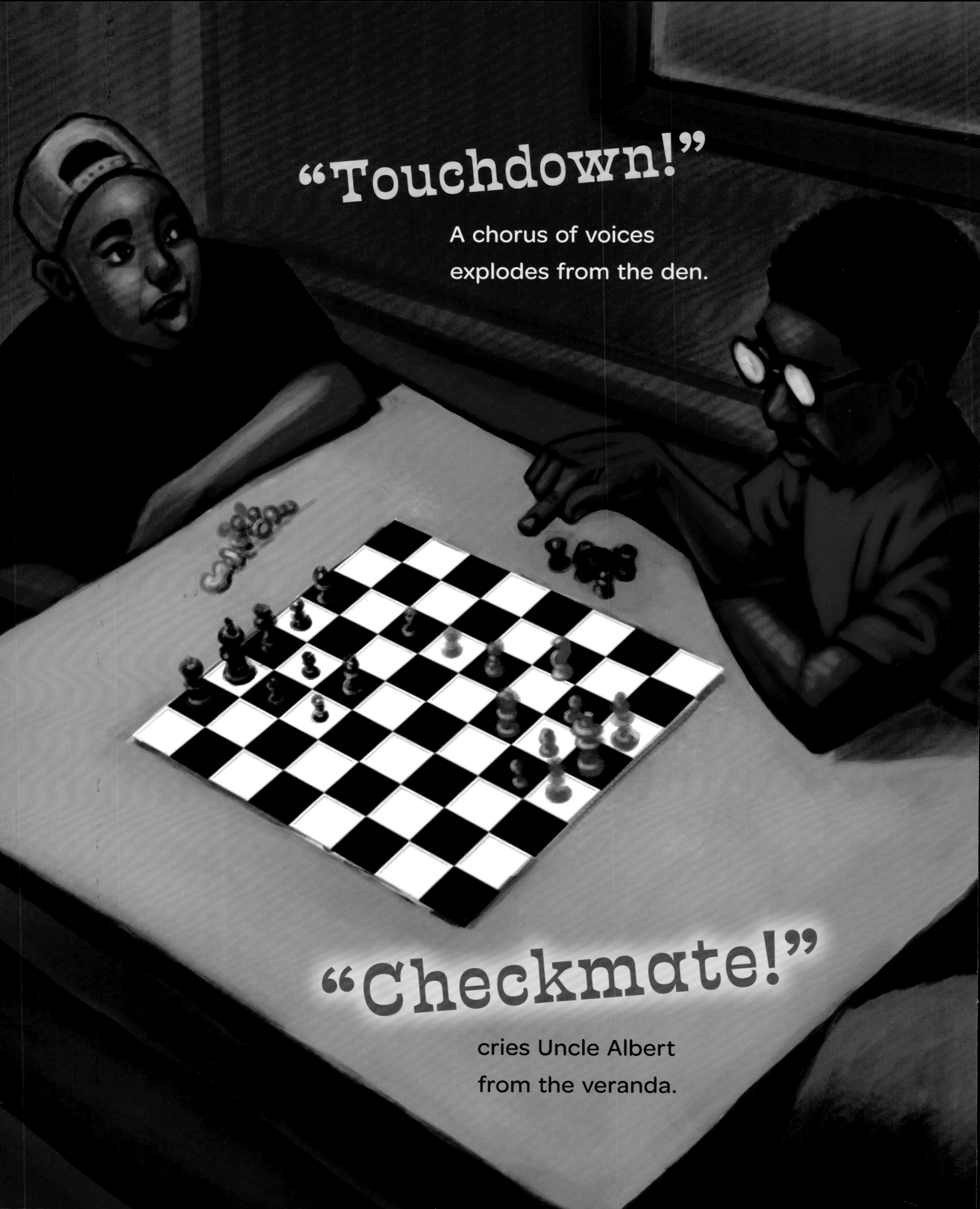

"Touchdown!"

A chorus of voices
explodes from the den.

"Checkmate!"

cries Uncle Albert
from the veranda.

Uncle Wesley tries to let me win
at checkers.
I am wise to that trick.
The game always ends in a draw.

Hopscotch erupts
on the driveway.
Rocks skip
across chalk boundaries.

The clang of horseshoes
and the dull thud of croquet mallets
reverberates in the shade
of hundred year old willow trees
dancing in the gentle breeze.

The aromas
of sizzling chicken
and frying hair
float from the kitchen.
Aunt Audrey always uses
too much grease on both.

I slurp on homemade lemonade,
tart and sassy. Uncle Wesley sips sweet tea
spiced with fresh mint from the garden.

"Need more sugar?" Uncle Wesley asks.

"Yes!" I say.
He kisses me on the cheek.
I blush ruby red.

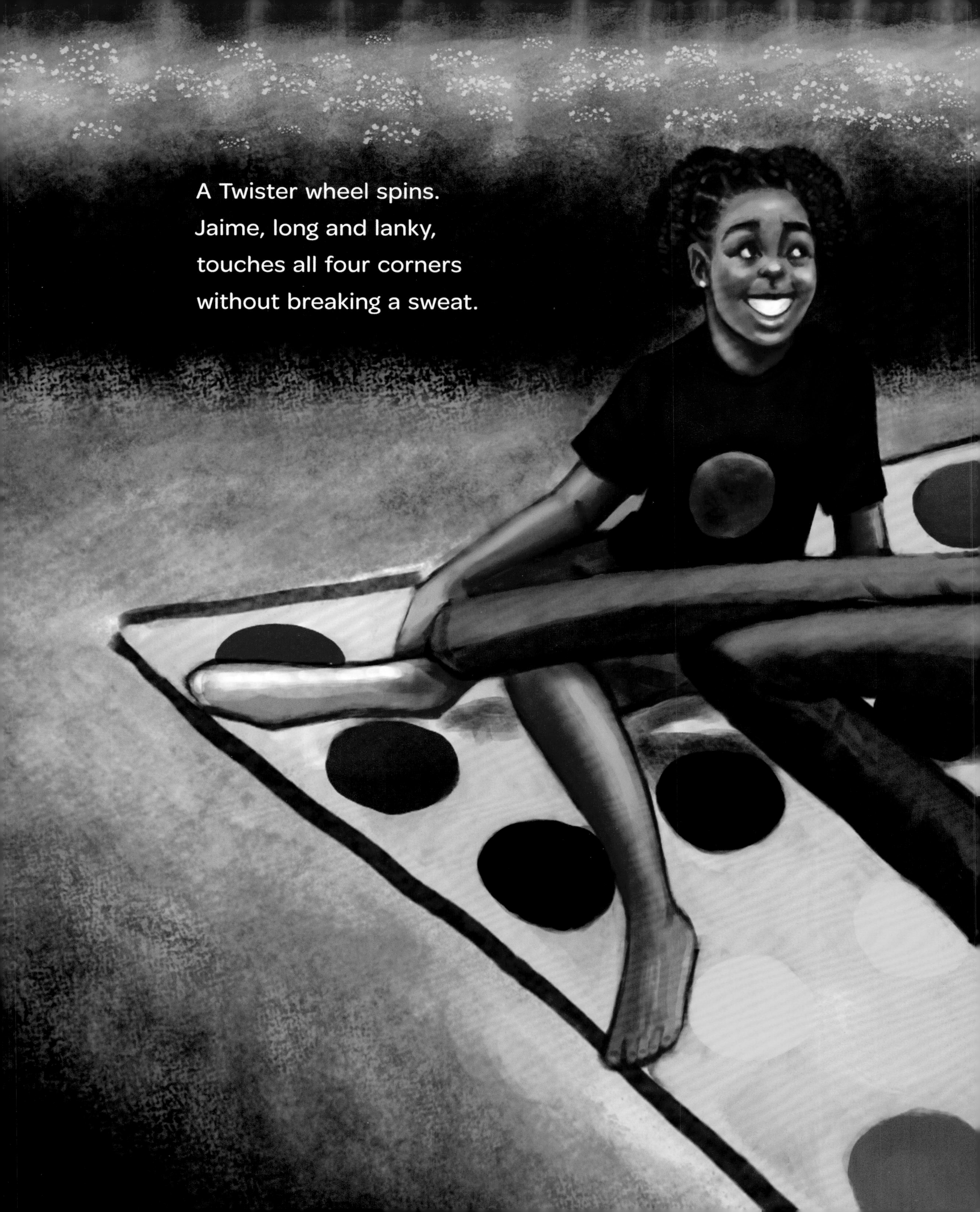

A Twister wheel spins.
Jaime, long and lanky,
touches all four corners
without breaking a sweat.

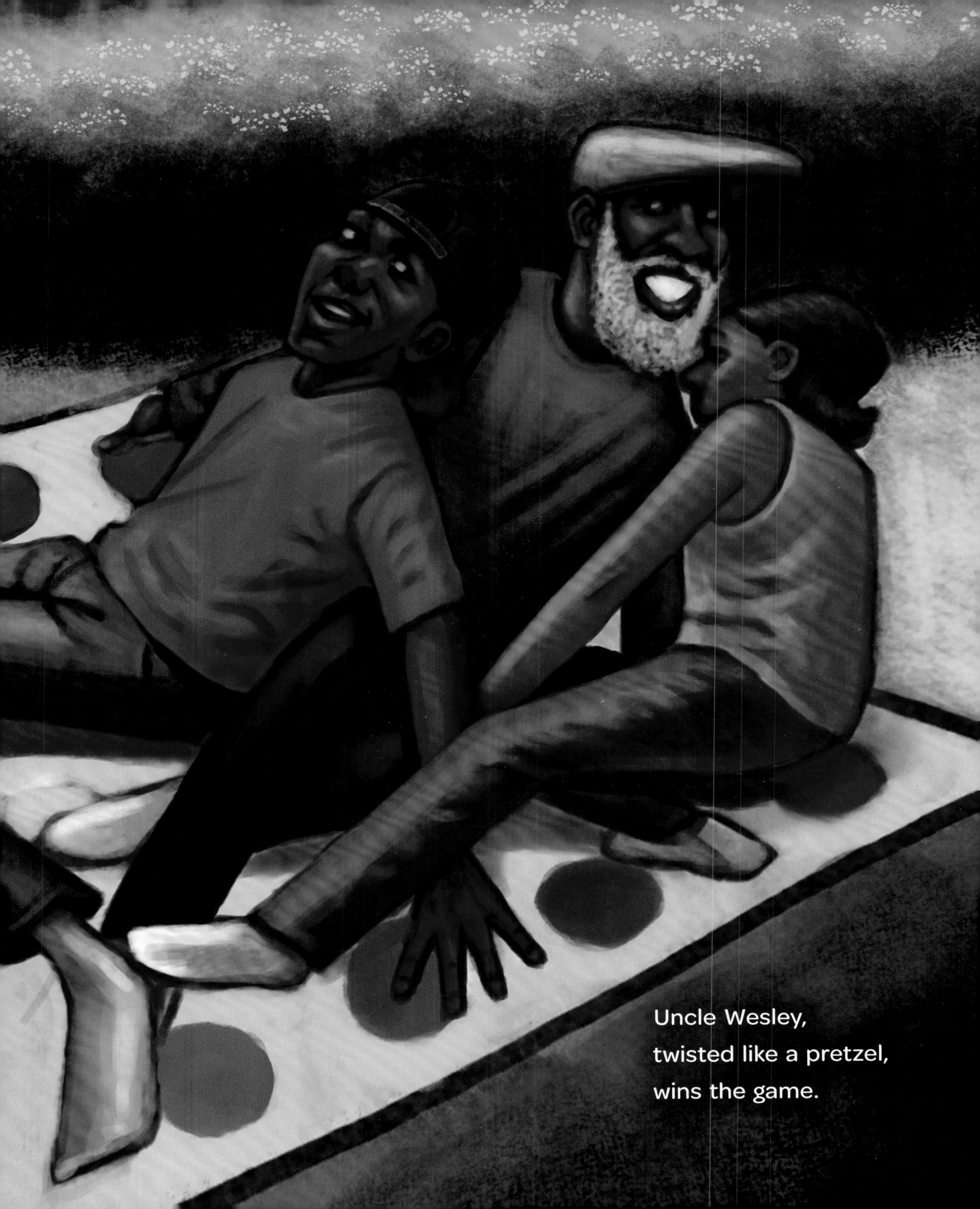

Uncle Wesley,
twisted like a pretzel,
wins the game.

Brandon gets out ropes,
tangled like old ivy vines.

"You rest," I say,
as Uncle Wesley puts things right.

"I may be old, Sara Jane Johnson,
but I've still got a lot of life in me!"

And shows us how
Double-Dutch jumping is done.

It's not long before the annual debate starts
over who makes the best catfish,
how much fatback to put in the greens
and how to get the lumps
out of Granny Josephine's gravy recipe.

Food flies.

Cheryl says Linda's hat
blocks the sun for miles.

"You wish **you** looked this good!"

Linda shouts
as she storms across the lawn.

She's easy to spot in the crowd.
She wears so much eye shadow,
when she blinks
it looks like headlights
on high beam.

The slap of cards on the table
echoes across the lawn.

"Ace beats a king!"
screams Bobby.

"Cheater!"
yells his brother Billy.

Aunt JoAnne uses all of her tiles
on a word no one can find
in the dictionary.
Letters shower across the patio
like hail.

TENSIONS flare.

FEELINGS boil.

“This is the wrong kind of ruckus for a party,”
Uncle Wesley whispers.
“Who’s going to put things right once I’m gone?”

I smile a sly smile,
crank up the music,
and hold out my hand.
"Would you like to dance?"

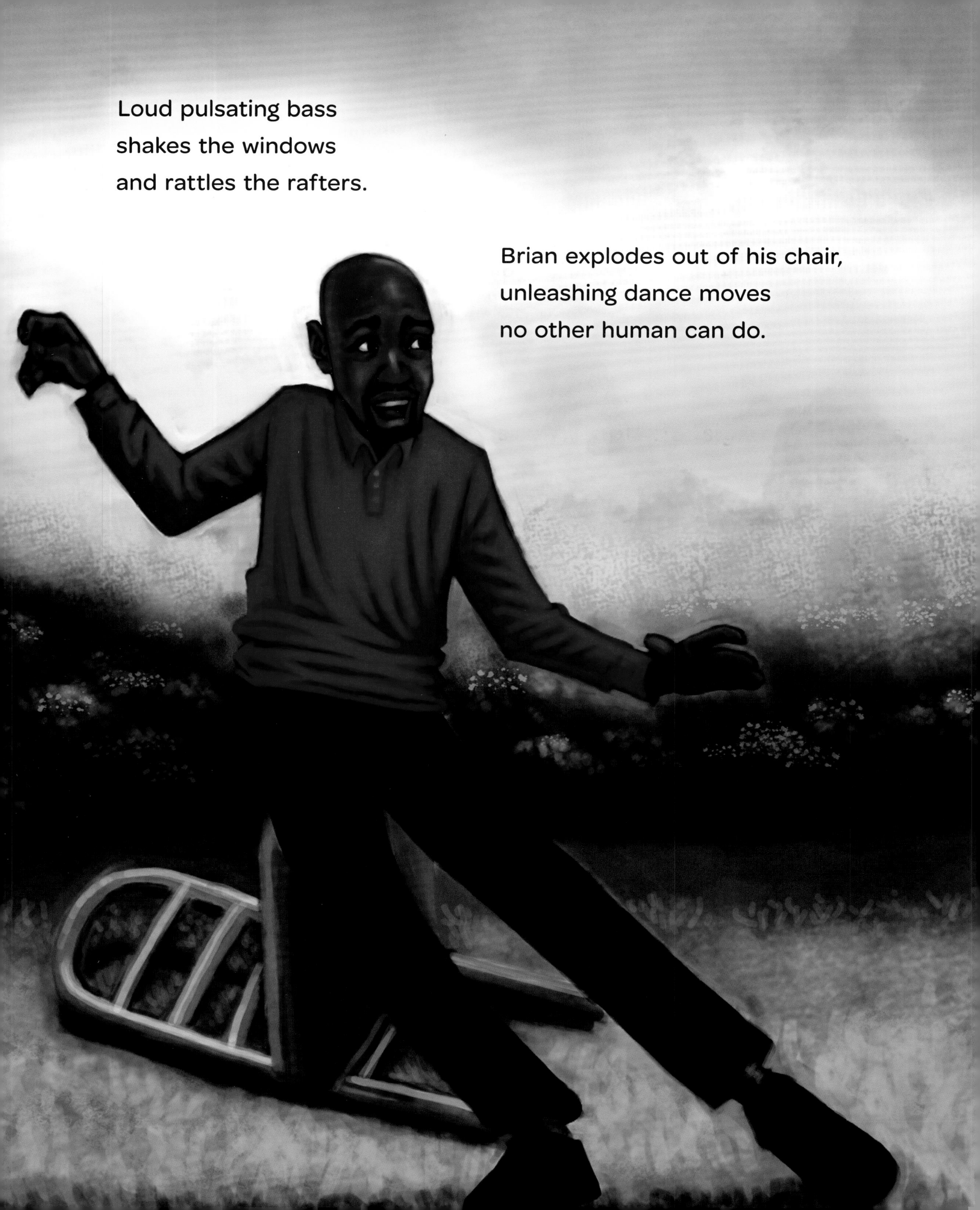

Loud pulsating bass
shakes the windows
and rattles the rafters.

Brian explodes out of his chair,
unleashing dance moves
no other human can do.

Aunt Vicki joins him,
showing off her signature steps.

“Good work,” Uncle Wesley whispers.

As he and I

start an Electric Slide.

Soon everyone is on their feet,
trying to outdo each other.
Hips, legs, and arms
fly in every direction.

And soon

comes the sweet sound of laughter.

... Johnson laughter.

Suddenly thunder cracks
in the distance.

The party is ruined.

But the family…

keeps on dancing.